BLACKLIST HOOKUP

SADIE HALLER

QTP

Copyright © 2020 by Sadie Haller

All rights reserved.

No part of this book may be reproduced in any form or by any electronic or mechanical means, including information storage and retrieval systems, without written permission from the author, except for the use of brief quotations in a book review.

ISBN: 978-0-9959811-4-0

ABOUT THIS BOOK

Looking to hook up with a kinky fellow celebrity near you when nobody—literally nobody—can know you're the opposite of vanilla?

There's an app for that.

Quietly warn a fellow actress not to be alone with a certain producer and... BOOM. I'm dumped from Hollywood's A-list to everyone's blacklist in the blink of an upload. So when I accidentally swipe right on my ex, who is still very much a hot commodity in this town, I'm not about to tank his career along with mine. But Eli has questions, and I just might like the way he plans to wring the answers out of me.

Fetwrk is a hook-up app for the debauched and kinky. More whips and chains than hearts and flowers.

BOOKS BY SADIE HALLER

Dominant Cord

One Gold Heart

One Gold Knot

One Gold Triquetra

Tainted Pearl

Tainted Shadow

Power Brokers

Chief of Perversion

Agent of Denial (Coming soon)

Fetwrk

Power Exchange

Blacklist Hookup

Unfriendly Relations

Frisky Beavers

Prime Minister

Dr. Bad Boy

Full Mountie

Mr. Hat Trick

PROLOGUE

Eli

"I SIMPLY CANNOT WAIT to become a great-great-aunt. I just know you two will make the most beautiful children."

I barely manage to swallow my mouthful of wine without choking.

I don't dare look at Calli, because neither of us will be able to keep a straight face. Everything between us is a fabrication, straight out of the studio's publicity department.

We've just finished filming *First Last Kiss* together, and have been fake dating to add to the hype.

It's beyond laughable.

The thing is, Auntie Gert was so thrilled about me dating Calliope Muir, I didn't have the heart to disappoint her. I figured Calli and I would split amicably and remain good friends before there was a risk of her meeting any of my family, but my great-aunt has a way of bulldozing you into doing what she wants. And she wanted Calli to join us for dinner.

"Miss Simmons—"

"Now, now, Calli, none of that formal bullshit. You're family. Auntie Gert will do just fine."

Family? Oh Jesus.

"Auntie Gert, I think you're still a bit young to be adding another *great* don't you? Surely you want to live a little before you're saddled with another generation of whippersnappers?"

I could just about kiss Calli right now. I've not brought many actual girlfriends, let alone a fake one, to meet my great-aunt, but damn if she isn't the first one to go toe-to-toe with her.

"Eli, you didn't tell me she was such a charmer."

That's not all I haven't told you. "I thought you'd like to discover some of her virtues on your own." *Because apparently, she has some I didn't know about.*

"Auntie Gert, I hate to say it—"

"But you need to go. I understand, dears." She lets out a big, drama-queen sigh. "Young love. I remember those days. Things getting hot and heavy in the backseat—"

Calli coughs to hide her amusement, and I frantically text my great-aunt's driver.

"Oh, Calli dear, that cough sounds terrible. I do hope you aren't coming down with something."

"No, I'm fine. Just a tickle in the throat."

"Thank heavens. Now, I'd like a photo of the two of you, please."

I put my arm around Calli, and we both smile at the phone Auntie Gert is holding up.

"No, no, that won't do. Kiss her Eli. I want something real, not that practised for the fans nonsense."

In all our fake dating, we've never actually kissed.

Calli and I look at each other, and I lean in to give her my best screen kiss.

Except...damn.

I prepare to take another longer taste.

"Perfect. Uploading to Instagram now."

I yank back and stare at my great-aunt in horror and amazement. I forgot just how enthusiastically she gloms onto technology. God help me if she ever discovers the Fetwrk app.

Just before she gets into her car, Auntie Gert hauls me in for a hug. "I like this one, my boy. Don't fuck it up."

"She's feisty," Calli says once we're alone.

"That she is. I remember the first time I heard her drop the f-bomb. I was about eight. She told me it was her *special* word. Pro-tip—that explanation does not get f-bomb-dropping eight-year-olds out of trouble.

"I'm sorry for any discomfort this evening. I thought she'd behave. She—"

"No, actually, she was refreshing and an absolute delight. So, thank you for the entertaining evening," Calli says with a sweet smile.

Calli

I watch my career explode on live television with a morbid fascination borne of utter disbelief.

Who knew a quiet warning to a fellow actor, a warning that most certainly did not violate the non-disclosure agreement I signed, would launch a thermonuclear attack? It's not even like I gave her fucking details. I literally only suggested she might want to avoid being alone with her film's producer, Felix Alexander. I left out the part about him being an evil scumbag. And I definitely left out every last disgusting thing he did to me before forcing me to sign that NDA.

I'd read that fucking agreement forwards, backwards, and sideways. I thought I was safe, provided I adhered to both the letter and the spirit. And I have, as far as the law is concerned. Unfortunately, he played dirty.

Clip after clip showing me participating in various sex acts—conveniently shot at angles that ensure Felix's anonymity—play non-stop on almost every channel. Some of the cable channels don't even bother to pixelate my breasts or genitals.

Mortified doesn't even begin to describe it.

My phone rings, and it's my agent. One of the few contacts my phone is set to override my do not disturb for.

"Hey Janet, what's up?" I keep my voice upbeat, like my day couldn't be going better.

"Cut the bullshit happy-tude, Calliope. Your life and career are a shit-show. You're burned beyond recognition. Be in my office at three this afternoon." The call is disconnected before I can even respond.

I'm not an idiot. I know damned well Janet is doing the agent equivalent of firing me this afternoon in the splashiest way she can—by making me come to her, forcing me to run the gauntlet of reporters and photographers looking to get a sound bite or an unflattering photo.

And once I leave, she'll issue a diplomatic press release along the lines of *us coming to a mutual decision to sever our professional relationship.*

I spend the morning doing everything I can think

of to take care of myself. I start with a romance novel and a long, hot bubble bath because I need whatever happy-ever-after I can get.

I don't bother making an effort to look pretty for the press. Fuck 'em. Like Janet said, I'm burned. Even if I did tart myself up, they'll make sure to print me looking like shit.

At two, I open my front door, ready to face my future, and I'm feeling feisty. After publicly releasing sex tapes featuring me—that I wasn't aware he'd taken —I really don't think he has much left in his arsenal. All the nasty, disgusting things he got me to do? None of them were illegal.

I'm bombarded with shouted questions. Each more demeaning than the last. I hold up my hands and wait for quiet.

"I will not be taking questions. If I am interrupted while giving my statement, I will immediately stop talking and leave. Understood?"

There's a lot of nodding and some mutterings.

"For those who are wondering if that's really me in those clips, the answer is yes. Was I aware I was being filmed? Absolutely not. That footage was taken entirely without my knowledge or consent. Were the acts I participated in consensual? That depends on your definition. I won't name the other person in the video because I am bound by a non-disclosure agreement, but I can guarantee you, I'm not the only woman he's taken advantage of." I take a long, shaky breath. If he has film of me, he has film of every other woman he's coerced into performing sex acts. And as abhorrent as that is, I take the tiniest bit of solace in knowing I've just tipped them off. "Recently, I warned a young woman not to be alone with this man. That wasn't a violation of the NDA I signed, so he had no legal redress. Instead, he retaliated by publicly humiliating me. Revenge porn is illegal in this state, but as with all things, rich, powerful white men in this country tend to operate outside the law with impunity."

And with that, I stalk off to my car. It's almost amusing seeing them race for their own vehicles, so they can follow me. Some will succeed. Some may even know where I'm going. No matter, they've got all they're getting from me.

I just hope they decide to air it.

ONE

Eli

As soon as I walk into the hotel ballroom, my phone vibrates. I pull it far enough from my pocket to see it's just another Fetwrk notification, and I dismiss it the same way I've done with all the others.

I still can't get used to this shit.

Looking to hook up with a compatible kinky fellow celebrity near you?

There's an app for that.

Not that I've actually done anything with said app, yet. But I'm getting close to desperate. The closest I've been to fucking anyone, let alone indulging my kinky side, was when I kissed Calli at dinner.

Last time I got my freak on was a huge mistake in judgement. Lucky for me, my manager, David Carr, has connections, and the sticky situation I found myself in disappeared quickly, albeit expensively. And it's money I would have spent many times over without a second thought for the magic Mel Seymour worked.

When my career started to take off, Dave sat me down and made it very clear that he was to be my first phone call if I ever found myself in a bind. And if I didn't follow his instructions to the letter, I could kiss both him as my manager, and my career as a Hollywood A-lister goodbye.

After that debacle was out of the way, Mel set me up with this app. What is it they say, once bitten, twice shy? I'd met Tara Langston at the play party of a friend of a friend. I made the mistake of thinking that meant the rest of the players were trustworthy.

Now I have an app that all but guarantees the other members are safe to play with.

So, yeah, I've been lurking for the past few months. But the longer I go without getting my kink on, the stronger the urge is to call off this sham of a relationship with Calli and take advantage of the potential playmate in my pocket.

But she's had a pretty rough go of it since that video of her hit, our romance seems to be continuing to maintain some public support, and it makes my Auntie Gert happy. I refuse to acknowledge the fact that I like her and enjoy spending time with her. So, for now, I'm sticking with the fake dating.

"Eli! Glad you could make it." Jude Anderson stands grinning in front of me, and as I shake his outstretched hand, he pulls me in for a bro-hug.

"The only time you're glad to see me is when you're hard up for a wingman."

"Not true, my friend." I raise an eyebrow, and he shrugs. "Okay, sometimes true. But not tonight."

"Because...?"

"I nailed down the attendee to my own personal after-party five minutes after I got here."

"Jesus, Jude," I say, shaking my head.

"What?"

"You're going to find yourself in deep shit if you're not careful." *Don't ask me how I know.*

"Don't worry. It's mutually assured destruction."

And with those last three words, my concern evaporates. 'Mutually assured destruction' is exactly how Fetwrk was explained to me. A social network that connects people who have everything to lose and nothing to gain by outing their hook-ups.

I nod slowly. "Good to know."

Five fucking minutes.

That's all it took for Jude to find himself a good time with a safe happy fucking ending for the night.

Those notifications on my phone are now burning

a big hole in my pocket, but as far as the rest of the world is concerned, I'm dating. And that means I spend more time with my lubed-up fist.

I shake off that thought as we're joined by Jordan Cage, a guitarist in some band I can never remember the name of, and Prince Duncan, the youngest son of the King of England and consummate playboy. The conversation immediately turns to super cars because we've all got them, and strong opinions on which is the best.

I'm surprised when, out of the corner of my eye, I see Calli walk in. She was supposed to be at some other party, which is why I'm here stag. And why I left that app running on my phone.

TWO

Calli

I DON'T EVEN KNOW why I'm here. I have always despised these stupid events, yet I pulled in a very valuable favor to get an invite to this shindig because I got disinvited from a different party, and my life is all about being seen. When your acting career is at some state of mid-flush down the toilet, held by a filament only because you're fake-dating Hollywood's golden boy, you'll do whatever it takes to catch a break.

Huh...I guess I do know why I'm here.

My gaze slides to Eli. He really is beyond hot. He could have his pick of women, single or married, and never worry about how it will affect his career, yet he's kept this bullshit thing going with me.

I'm both grateful to him for providing the cushion below my very long fall, and angry as fuck that the only reason I can get facetime with anyone at all is because of my connection to him.

Welcome to the inequality that is Hollywood.

I consider taking advantage of my *relationship* with Eli and joining his group. But I've always been one to make my own way, and I'd rather not have to rely on a man to move me along in the world.

But fuck me, given a real chance, I'd totally do Eli. It's not like the world doesn't think I already am. Along with god knows how many other men. I know they're all looking down their noses at me, all the while looking for more videos of me to justify their disdain.

Grabbing a glass of champagne I don't intend to drink, I make my way slowly through the room, lingering at the fringes of various groups in the hopes of joining in, and moving on to the next when it becomes clear I won't be acknowledged, but before it becomes awkward.

It's a fine line, and I walk it really, really well.

Until someone behind me calls me a whore under their breath as they walk past.

That's when I give in to my pride and sidle up to the group Eli and Jude are in. Because why the fuck not? At least I can count on Eli to acknowledge my existence. Then I can end my night on a high-ish note, go home, and soak in a hot bath overflowing with raspberry scented bubbles and a good book.

I seem to be doing that a lot lately. Oh well, it's a lot healthier than a drinking problem.

They're talking about super cars, and I have thoughts. So many fucking thoughts, but I keep them in my head where they belong. Nobody wants to know what I think about anything.

Not anymore.

Eli smiles at me as I approach and slides his arm over my shoulders.

"Calliope. You did that series, *Chix 'n Cars* a while back, you must have an opinion," he says.

I can feel the red hot burn of embarrassment radiating over my skin as the group turns as one to stare at me, making me feel that awful 'alone on the stage with the big follow-spot shining on you and you've forgotten your line' panic.

I should have slipped away while I had a chance. But I didn't, so my best option now is to put them off and beat a hasty retreat.

"Well, actually," I start with the classic mansplainer opening, because how often does that opportunity arise? "I don't really have anything to add to the discussion." I lock gazes with Eli, silently pleading for him to just drop it. And what the fuck was I thinking? Wanting to get noticed? Other people within earshot are staring with disdain. Like I'm shit someone's brought in on the sole of their shoe.

"Come on, you spent months doing that show," he goads. "And I know damned well you did a ton of research."

And I officially hate Eli Simmons with the intensity of a thermo-nuclear meltdown. He may be awfully pretty to look at, and reasonably good company, but when he pressed the issue like that—I hit peak fuck-it and let loose.

"Once upon a time ago, I may have had some thoughts, but my poor teensy widdle brain can only hang on to information for so long before it's replaced by more important stuff like remembering to steam-clean my vagina on the regular before filling it with jade to keep it tight so needle-dicked assholes can feel like they're Dirk Diggler along with other bullshit beauty tips that the world would be better off without."

I turn and stalk towards the exit, downing my champagne and depositing my empty glass on a tray enroute.

I make it to the main foyer of the hotel before a hand closes around my biceps. I turn sharply and glare into the most beautiful fucking grey eyes on the planet.

Eli.

"I'm sorry."

"Don't be. Now if you don't mind..." I look pointedly to his hand.

As soon as he removes it, I continue walking away.

THREE

Eli

Fᴜᴄᴋ. Me.

The road to hell, and all that.

I'd watched her as she made her way around the room. People turning away from her as she approached. Not giving her their backs but turning far enough to make their point.

Rejection after rejection. And with each one, her shoulders slumped just a little lower, even though she kept her chin up high.

I've never seen anything like it. And it makes me wonder whether I've never been exposed to that kind of thing before or whether I've been completely clueless and only aware because it's happening to someone I care about.

It was obvious that joining me was her last-ditch effort, and I thought trying to include her in a conversation on a subject she was infinitely more qualified to discuss than any of us were would be a good way show the rest of the room how to behave.

Clearly I misread something.

I followed her as far as the foyer, before realizing that chasing after her would turn this into a media circus and wind up front and center on every single tabloid and gossip site there is. There's already a very real risk there is footage courtesy of any number of vipers who wouldn't think twice to throw us under the bus if it meant a chance to further themselves.

Maybe it's time to cut Calli loose. Even though everything between us is supposed to be fake, I still feel like a total shit. I'll call her in the morning to officially break things off and discuss a press statement. And then I'd better call Auntie Gert.

There's no way I want to go back in the ballroom, but I'm not ready to go home, so I head straight to the hotel bar, order a Coke, and pull out my phone. I'm ready to see what Fetwrk has to offer.

FOUR

Calli

I STOP JUST before I reach the hotel's VIP entrance and take my phone from my purse to text for my car. The Fetwrk icon jumps out at me. My agent—ex-agent —gave it to me at our last meeting when we cut ties.

"If I'd known you were into kinky sex, I'd have made sure you had this. Consider it my parting gift."

As far as I'm concerned, Eli and I are done, so there's nothing stopping me from trying it out.

If I were smart, I'd probably hold off for a few days, but I'm fed up with being on my best behavior.

I touch the icon, and seconds later, Fetwrk is making my phone vibrate so much I'm tempted to just shove it down the front of my panties and guarantee a happy ending.

However, it's been so long since I've had any sort of physical human connection—with the exception of *the kiss*.

And sex...well, I imagine Eli would have been willing—he is a man, after all, and obviously, I'm not averse to casual sex, but I like it rough and primitive with a giant serving of *ouch*. And that's something I'm not going to get from someone respectable and scandal-free like Eli.

I start checking profiles of those located here in the hotel as I wonder if the general public has even the tiniest inkling of the sheer multitude celebrities who are seriously off-the-chart perverts.

I decide on SatisFetion, swipe right, and wait to see if he accepts. A message pops up on my screen.

SATISFETION: In the hotel bar, table near the back to the right of the door.

JUST OUTSIDE THE DOOR, I message back to let him know I'm on my way in and wearing a red dress.

It's crowded, but the tables are well spaced and it's easy to see who I'm looking for. My excitement withers on the vine as I spot my date.

Eli.

I try to leave before he sees me, but I'm too late. He catches my eye and I'm pinned in place by his knowing look.

FIVE

Eli

THAT LITTLE MINX.

All these months I could have been getting my kink on.

Don't you fucking move, I mouth to her as I cross the floor in long, purposeful strides.

"Oh no. You're not going to fucking stand me up. You and I—we're going somewhere very private and very soundproof right fucking now, because we've definitely got shit to work through."

"No. We can't. This was a mistake. I mean, we're done and—"

"What's your safeword?"

"Red. But that doesn't matter."

"Oh, it matters very fucking much because that's

the only way you're noping out of anything tonight. Now let's go."

With my hand at the base of her spine, I propel her gently, but firmly forward.

"You know you shouldn't play when you're angry," she says.

"You think I'm angry? No, not even close. If I were, you can bet we wouldn't be playing, but we'd sure as fuck still be talking."

"My car..."

"Will be fine. If necessary, I'll arrange for someone to get it home for you. Right now, you are mine, and after all the fucking nights I went home with blue balls, we've got a lot of time to make up for."

"This is a really bad idea. Of all the people in the world, really, I'm not the one—"

"Oh, you are exactly the one. Now, no more arguing with me. From here on out, you'll just earn yourself punishments. And I've read your profile. I know exactly what you'll take but not enjoy."

"I can get them to bring my car and I'll follow—"

"Did you think I was kidding? That's one. Do you want to earn more, or do you want to have a good time? I'm going to have fun, either way. Safeword is your only salvation. If you don't say red, then I'm not stopping until we're both thoroughly satisfied. Got it?"

"Yeah."

"Is that really how you want this to go, because that's two."

"I'm sorry, Sir."

Once we're in the car, I take some time to calm down and think.

"Calli, the way I see it, we have two options. We date for real with all the kinky benefits. Or this is a one and done thing and we both move on. The choice is yours."

"Do I need to give you an answer right now?"

"No. But soon." I leave it at that, and we finish the drive in silence.

SIX

Calli

"Where are we?" I ask as we pull up to a gated property in Hidden Hills.

"Depends on my mood. Sometimes it's my sanctuary. Tonight, it's my lair."

"You bring all your Fetwrk hookups here?"

"Nope. Just you."

"Why?"

"Because I want absolute privacy."

I think there's more to it than that, but right now, we're in a scene, and I'm already racking up punishments. And he's right, there's a lot on my limit list that I'll do but won't enjoy.

Fucking soft limits.

I really should redo that list and maybe slide some over to the hard side. Except it's more important to be completely honest about stuff when playing casually. Because if they can't trust that you really mean it with the hard limits, then they're going to cross lines you don't ever want crossed.

Recalling the horror that is Felix Alexander, I will myself not to shudder.

Eli parks the car in the garage and leads me through a hallway to what proves to be his very well-equipped dungeon.

"Strip and neatly fold your clothes. You can leave them on there," he says, pointing to a wooden ladder-back chair near the door. "Then go stand facing the Saint Andrew's Cross."

I quickly undress. He gave no indication he wants a slow and sultry seduction. He said he wasn't angry, at least not so angry it would be dangerous for him to play, but he's definitely got a bug up his ass, and while I'm looking for a lot of rough and a fair bit of ouch, I'm not looking to push him without any idea of how far he's capable of going.

The only safe part of this is that of the two of us, he's the one who can least afford to be found out.

"As long as you remain perfectly still, I won't restrain you. At least not for this."

I clutch the handles on the upper part of the cross and spread my legs, so my feet are just inside the lower bits.

The falls of a flogger caress the skin across my shoulders, down my back, and up again, making me shiver.

"We could both use a little warm up."

He starts slow and gentle—over my shoulders, down my ass, across my shoulders—each pass a little firmer, warming my skin and making it tingle.

When he stops, I whimper complaint and receive a sharp flick of the flogger between my legs that makes me hop.

"Honestly, one tiny flogger swat to the pussy, and you lose all self-control. That is rather disappointing. I guess restraints will be necessary after all."

He's disappointed, and I don't like being the cause.

"I'm sorry, Sir."

"Don't worry, you will be." I hold out my wrists as he fastens leather cuffs. "I'd love to get the rope out, but to do it justice, I'd require more time than we have tonight."

My belly quivers at the idea of rope. I love being tied up, but rarely have the pleasure because casual kinky sex doesn't often allow the time and patience for beauty.

Once my ankles are cuffed, he clips me to the cross.

Pressing himself against my back, he growls in my ear. "The only choice you get tonight is whether you take everything I give you or safeword out. That said, I will do my damnedest to take you to your limit but not beyond."

"Thank you, Sir."

He uses a Wartenberg wheel to trace patterns all over my back, making me flinch whenever he presses a little harder.

His deep chuckle sends a fluttering low in my belly. The sharp nip on my earlobe makes my pussy throb and ache.

"I'm going to spell something, and you're going to tell me what it is when I'm done. I'll be nice and do it in all capitals. Ready?"

"Yes, Sir."

"First letter."

The first stroke is straight down, then a diagonal down to the right. Another to the left, then one more straight down.

"M."

"Second letter."

Straight down. Bar across the top left to right. Another across the bottom.

"I."

"Third."

Straight down. Downward diagonal to the right, and another straight down.

"N."

"Last one."

Straight down. To the right from that at the top. Another to the right farther down, and one more below that.

"E."

"Do you think you have it?"

"Yes, sir. Mine."

"Absolutely mine." The way he says it. Having it written on my back—for the short time the marks will remain—makes me feel gooey inside. Almost like...I shut down those thoughts. This is a scene. Nothing more.

He unfastens me from the cross and propels me across the room.

"On your back." He pats the top of a hip-high bondage bench. As I lay down, he pulls and pushes me until he's satisfied with my position, then clips my wrists and ankles to the sides and places a ball in my hand.

"Dropping that will make me stop and check in. But unless you say your safeword, it won't necessarily mean I won't start again. Understood?"

"Yes, Sir."

"Open."

I open my mouth, and he straps a ring gag on. Holding my head, he releases the board that was supporting it, and gently lowers it until he's got a straight shot for his cock into my throat.

I've deep throated—the world has seen me, thanks to Felix Alexander and the video that just won't die—but damn, not in this position with a gag. I feel a little panicked, but deep down, this is what I want.

Because this is what Eli wants.

And it's not a hard limit. Not even close.

His cock comes closer to my mouth, and I close my eyes, determined to take this with all the poise and dignity I can muster. Because I want this to be good for him. I want it to be good for me. Because this may be the one and only real-life hookup he and I will be having.

He slides his cock along my tongue, and as the tip hits my soft palate, I swallow against it, willing my gag-reflex to stand down.

It doesn't cooperate and my shoulders burn from strain as my gut heaves. He presses harder, ignoring my body's reaction to the intrusion, not stopping until he's all the way in.

"Look at you, taking it all down for me. What a good girl."

This is the first time tonight he's told me I'm good, and it makes me stupidly happy enough to grin around the gag and his cock.

He pulls all the way back, and I catch a quick breath before he surges forward, holding himself deep as I struggle to swallow against the gagging and heaving.

"We're going to be here for a while, so you may as well give in and let it happen."

That's exactly what I'm trying to do, but he's got a big cock, and my throat has other ideas.

He pulls back, letting me catch my breath again. "I'm going to skull fuck you, so you're going to have to catch a breath where you can, because I'm not stopping until I come down your throat or you drop that ball."

And that's all the warning I get before he braces his hands at the back of my head and plunges into my throat hard and deep, over and over. As savage as he is, every single stroke comes out far enough for me to catch a little air.

Every. Single. One.

My gag reflex has settled down—run away in terror more like. And suddenly, I'm confident I can do this.

He speeds up and I can feel his cock as it swells just that little bit more.

"Here it comes. Be a good girl and take it all." Like I have a choice.

Two final plunges, and then he holds my head tight against him, his cock pulsing inside my throat as he comes.

My lungs are burning by the time he pulls out.

"Such a good girl for me." He removes the gag and unclips the cuffs, then picks me up and lays me gently on the bed in the corner. "Have a little rest while I get some things ready."

I try to watch what he's doing, to prepare myself for what awaits me, but my eyelids are so heavy, and I'm worn out. I just can't stay awake.

"Wake up sleepyhead." Soft lips pepper my face with kisses, and I'm a little disoriented when I see Eli. Then it comes back to me.

"I'm sorry. How long was I asleep?"

"Only about half an hour. I wanted to let you sleep longer, but I wanted to do despicable things to you more." He shoots me what I'm sure he thinks is an evil grin, but really, it's just crooked and endearing.

Not that I'll ever tell him that.

"What kind of despicable things?" I ask.

"The kind that you'll thank me for because afterward you're going to come so hard you won't be able to think straight."

"I've heard that one before." Sadly, it's true, but in this case, I'm fairly certain he's a man who can absolutely back up his braggadocio.

"That's three."

"I was a good girl. You said so."

"Yes, you were a very good girl, but that doesn't cancel out punishments. And as cute as that smart mouth is, it has no place in a scene with me."

SEVEN

Eli

Her submission has been so complete and perfect, I have to check myself because I could easily get lost in top space.

I wasn't bullshitting when I told her I wanted to do every despicable thing I could think of. And her limits don't restrict me in any meaningful way.

I want to use her throat again. And rougher this time.

But she could decide this is a one and done deal, and I want to use as much of her as I can in the precious time I have left with her.

"Back to the bench. This time, on your stomach."

I clip her cuffs to the D-rings and check her circulation. "Everything okay?"

"Yes, Sir."

"Safeword?"

"Red, Sir."

"Use it if you need to." I don't expect her to need to, but I'm huge on consent. Even my most brutal non-con scenes have always been based on some level of consent, and the ability to revoke it at any time. "Before we start, is there any chance marks on your ass and upper thighs could be a problem for you in the next week or so?"

She rolls her eyes. "Hardly."

"And there's that smart mouth again."

"No, Sir. Marks won't be a problem. Anywhere."

Even though she just gave me free rein, I'm only going after her fleshiest parts. And for the next week or so, I'll glory in the knowledge she's feeling my marks every time she sits down.

"No warmup. I'm still feeling mean, and I think deep down, you need hard, fast, and painful."

"Yes please, Sir."

"The room is sound-proof, so scream if you need to." Taking my position, I touch the cane to her ass and shift a bit before drawing my arm back and letting loose with the first stripe.

Her silence both surprises and irritates me. I want to hear her screams. Another stroke, harder this time, and across her mid-thighs. Again, no response, and I have to tamp down my irrational irritation at her incredible self-control.

"Calliope, did someone train you to remain silent?"

"Yes, Sir."

Motherfucker. Taking a deep breath, I count to ten, then let it out slowly.

"Were you trained to give your Dom what he wants?"

"Yes, Sir."

"Is he your Dom?"

"No, Sir."

"Who is your Dom."

"You, Sir."

"Damned straight. Now, your Dom wants to hear your feelings. And what your Dom wants overrides all else."

"Yes, Sir."

I pull back and nail her mid-thigh again, and this time she lets out a scream that's music to my ears.

"Good girl."

I keep going with the cane until she's a sobbing, begging mess and her ass is a beautiful, multi-colored tangle of welts.

I really only have time to fuck her once before we call it a night, and as much as I'd love to fuck that tight little asshole of hers, I have other plans for it.

I give her a good hard smack on her ass, so she has

something to think about while I gather the necessaries for the final act.

Condom, lube, inflatable butt plug, and the Hitachi.

I give her butt another stinging swat before spreading her cheeks and applying some lube. She rotates her hips some, earning her another smack.

"Behave, or I'll change my plans."

She immediately goes still, and I slide the plug in with almost no effort. As soon as it's seated, I start pumping the bulb.

"This is going to get big. I want to make sure that cunt of yours makes me feel like Dirk Diggler."

When I decide the plug is inflated enough, I disconnect the air hose, grab the Hitachi, and press it against her clit.

As I position myself at her entrance, I flip the big vibrator to high and thrust my cock deep inside her.

"Come as much as you like. You've been a such a very good girl," I whisper in her ear as I press myself hard against her tender ass and thighs, rocking my hips in shallow bursts.

After her first orgasm, I let myself go, slamming into her, making her squeal each time I bottom out.

Whenever I get close to coming, I pull out and make her come twice. She's begging me not to make her come by the time I'm ready to take my own pleasure.

"No more, please. I'm done. I can't. Please, no more."

"You'll take what I give you."

Her sobs of resignation push me over the edge, and I empty myself into her.

Draped over her back, I rest and catch my breath for a few moments before I ditch the condom, unclip her, and carry her to the bed.

"You were such a good girl for me. Thank you."

Her face is a blotchy, mascara-smeared mess. Her eyes are swollen from crying, and she couldn't look more beautiful to me than in that moment.

"Thank you, Sir."

Wrapping my arms around her, I hold her tight against me and rest my chin on her head.

Eventually, I have to wake her because I have an early call and need to get us both home if I'm going to get any sleep before my ass is due in makeup.

"Time to get you home. I'll arrange to have your car brought there for you."

"No. Just drop me off at the hotel, and I'll be fine getting home on my own."

"Not an option."

"Eli, please. I can't explain why, but I just need to be able to drive myself home."

I give in, because I have no good reason not to. But that doesn't stop me from following her at a distance to make sure she gets home safely.

EIGHT

Calli

As soon as I get home, I strip down and admire all the pretty marks on my skin in the full-length mirror.

Everything feels swollen and hot and I want to do it over again.

All of it.

Everything Eli did. Everything he made me feel was right. Perfect. What I've been searching for. And the universe is just cruel enough to give me a tiny fucking taste, then snatch it all away.

My phone alerts me to a text. I want to ignore it. Nothing good ever comes in the darkest of night. But curiosity gets the better of me.

. . .

Eli: How do they look?

How THE FUCK does he know I'm admiring his handiwork?

Calli: Every bit as amazing as they feel.
   Eli: Excellent. Sweet dreams, good girl.

I CLIMB into bed and drift off to sleep.

When I wake, I feel the best I've felt in a really long time. I needed a good ass-beating and crying jag more than I realized. Time to give Eli my answer.

Calli: So, that question you asked me last night in the car…
   Eli: Have you made a decision?
   Calli: Can we go with option one and make it real?
   Eli: Absolutely.

I START HOUSE-HUNTING IN EARNEST.

There are a few in Pasadena that interest me, but I

have no idea how to go about buying a house anony-
mously. So I text Eli.

Call: How do you buy a house without anyone knowing?

I watch my phone for way too long. I try to forget the
text and spend the rest of the day Googling and cursing
the day I decided to act under my own name rather
than adopt a stage name. Though it probably wouldn't
matter much anyway because real names still wind up
on a public record.

If I had more money behind me, I could probably
do it as a corporation or something, but the reality is,
though my income is healthy and steady, it is limited.
Even buying a new house will be entirely dependent
on me selling the old one.

I'm eating my dinner, still Googling in vain, when
my phone buzzes.

Eli: You looking to move?
    **Calli: Yep. Waving the white flag. Time to
fade into obscurity.**
    Eli: Sit tight. I'll get back to you.

. . .

By the time his next text arrives, I've finished dinner, cleaned the kitchen, showered, and done a load of laundry. Ah, the glamorous life of a former Hollywood A-lister.

Eli: You're going to hear from Mel. Do exactly as she tells you, and she'll see you right.

He says Mel with no last name like I should know who the fuck that is. I don't bother asking.

Calli: Thank you.
    Eli: No problem

A few minutes later, my phone buzzes again.

Eli: How are you doing today? Too sore? Emotionally okay?
    Calli: I'm fine, thank you. All is good.

· · ·

BETTER THAN GOOD.

A couple of hours later, my phone alerts me to a text, and my heart races thinking maybe it's Eli again.

UNKNOWN: This is Mel Seymour. Calling you now.

THEN MY PHONE RINGS.

"Hello?"

"Calliope Muir?"

"Yes?" Even though Eli said I'd hear from someone called Mel, I've had enough encounters with the media to be leery.

"Hi, I'm Mel Seymour. Eli asked me to help you out with your accommodation issue. You're looking to relocate on the down-low?"

"Yes. I've got some places I'm interested in, but no idea what steps to take."

"Do you need to sell your current place to fund the new one?"

"Yes." Jesus, she's so curt, it's all I can do not to add *Ma'am.*

"I'm going to text you an email address. I want you

to send me links to all the listings you're interested in, and I'll get back to you in the next week."

"Thank you."

"It'll be fine. I promise."

And for no reason whatsoever, I believe her.

NINE

Eli

It's all I can do to keep myself from driving over to Calliope's house to see for myself that she's fine. And of course, if she is, then I'd want to do more evil things to her. And if she isn't, I'd want to hold her and coddle her until she's ready to take more of my devilment. I tell myself it's because I'm a responsible Dom because I don't want to admit that it's maybe something more.

At least I can do something to help with her living situation. I know she's not been able to get work for a while, and maybe money's tight. She wouldn't be the first rising star to get rich quick and not plan for rainy days.

Mel is the ultimate fixer, and the perfect solution to Calliope's problem.

It occurs to me that Mel should have been brought in back when the shit hit Calliope's fan. Any manager or agent worth their percentage knows Mel Seymour is the only call you make at the first sign of trouble.

Which leads me to think some fucker betrayed Calliope.

And that pisses me off.

I pull out my script and run my lines because I need a distraction and work is the only thing guaranteed to take my mind off of the most amazing scene I think I've ever had.

Hours later, I rub my neck and check the clock. Time for bed. Another early makeup call, and I'm already running a huge sleep deficit.

I resist the urge to call and hear her voice, but I can't go to sleep without saying good night.

ELI: Sweet dreams, good girl.

I DON'T EXPECT A RESPONSE, so I am stupidly pleased when she texts me back seconds later.

CALLIOPE: Thank you. You too.

• • •

I DON'T BOTHER to jack off, even though my dick is hard. Instead, I relive that part of my scene with Calliope where I hold back my own orgasm as she begs me not to make her come again.

I want to do that to her every night.

To hear her beg and plead and cry for me to stop making her come and doing it anyway because it's what I want.

I'm pretty sure nobody ever died from too many orgasms.

And then I want to do the opposite. Deny her for days on end while I come as often as I am physically able.

I want her skin always bearing new marks as my old ones change color and fade. I want her to scream in pain until she finally breaks and lets herself cry.

I want her.

The one woman in the world who could be perfect for me is neck deep in a career-destroying Hollywood scandal and trying to disappear. Meanwhile, I'm the golden boy whose photo shows up daily in any number of publications and gossip sites.

The thing is, there's got to be some way to make this work for us.

I give in to sleep, knowing tomorrow I'm going to be having my own chat with Mel.

TEN

Eli: Good morning. Pack a bag for two nights. A driver will pick you up at 3pm sharp. Be a good girl, and don't make him wait.

Calliope: What if I already have plans?

Not that I do.

Eli: That's one.

I guess that answers that.

My heart races. I wonder what he has planned. Two days scening in his dungeon? Or maybe something romantic like a quaint little bed and breakfast somewhere?

THREE O'CLOCK TAKES FOREVER to roll around. I've been ready to walk out the door since two. I lost count of how many times I changed my outfit before finally settling on jeans and a t-shirt because I have no idea what's in store, and it always helps if I'm feeling comfortable in my clothes.

I head straight outside as soon as I see the car arrive. There are a few paps lingering, shooting pictures, shouting questions.

"Calli, where are you going?"

"Where's Eli?"

I ignore them all as I climb into the car. Easier done when you don't know the answer. Their nagging voices are abruptly silenced as soon as the driver shuts the door.

It's not long before I recognize the route as the one Eli had driven that crazy, amazing night that seems like both yesterday and forever ago.

He's on the front steps waiting as the car comes through the gates and my belly is tied in knots. Last time I was here, he talked about wanting to use rope and wishing we had more time. Apparently, he's arranged for plenty of time.

As soon as the car and driver disappear back through the gates, Eli takes me by the hand and drags me into the house.

"Until ten tomorrow morning, you are mine to do with as I please. After that, we'll be looking at houses until dinner time. Leave your bag there for now and come with me."

I follow him through the house to the dungeon. "Strip, folded clothes on the chair. You will do this every time you enter this room unless I tell you otherwise."

"Yes, Sir."

I obey without hesitation because I'm not going to waste even a moment of our time together. If there's one thing I learned from my Hollywood downfall, it's to cherish every little gift because you never know when it might be snatched away.

"Good girl. Now stand for me, arms out front, legs wide." He buckles me into cuffs and I try to hide my disappointment. "Don't worry, we'll get to the rope eventually. But I have very specific plans for how each session begins. Now, on the bench on your back." I know what's coming, and I quiver in anticipation. "From now on, I don't expect to have to tell you what to do. After you strip, you will present for cuffs, then immediately take your place on the bench. Understood?"

"Yes, Sir."

He clips me to the sides of the bench and buckles me into the ring gag. "I'd like to get you to a point where I could trust that you could handle having me fuck your skull without the aid of the gag. Until then... this is how we roll." He presses the ball into my palm and I close my fingers around it. "Remember, if you drop, I stop. Got it?"

I nod and he lowers the neck support and slides his cock into my mouth.

I don't handle it any more gracefully than I did last time. I gag and heave and gasp for every breath until finally, his pulsing cock is buried deep in my throat as he empties himself into me. And I love every depraved second of it.

He raises the neck support and strokes my forehead. "I love making you gag and watching your stomach heave. It gets me even harder for you." He unclips me and carries me over to the bed. "You may have a little rest, but eventually, I want to work toward you going straight from a skull-fucking to whatever I have in store for you with no respite."

I like that he's talking about plans for the future. More than I probably should.

"On your belly. I've decided I want to look at the state of my marks while you rest."

I flip over, and my skin tightens as his hands skim over my flesh. "Lovely, but more faded than I'd hoped. Clearly, I'll need to go harder on you."

"Yes please, Sir."

His chuckle makes me feel content.

I'm just drifting when he takes my left arm and clips it to the headboard. I look up at him. "Back down and relax while you can."

Moments later, I'm attached facedown and spread-eagle to the bed.

From the corner of my eye, I see the evil Hitachi and I know what's coming. Well, who's coming, and that'll be me. Until I'm nothing but an unintelligible puddle of goo. And I shake my head frantically.

"That's two. You don't get to tell me no. That's not your safeword."

"I'm sorry, Sir."

"And yet, that will make exactly zero difference. I still owe you two from last time. No, I didn't forget. Bum up." I lift my hips as much as I can while Eli slips a pillow beneath me and secures the Hitachi in place. "You can relax now."

I lower myself and the head of the Hitachi is centered right on my clit.

As he pulls my ass cheeks apart, cold lube lands on

my back entrance and I wonder if he's that quick to recover or...

I can't tell whether the cold tip of the plug means it's glass or steel—not that it matters. It's going in my ass, and Eli isn't wasting any time.

"Take it for me. Relax, and take it like a good girl. Scream if it hurts."

It does hurt, but it's not scream-worthy just yet, and I won't pretend.

Not with him.

The pressure increases as he stretches me wider, and finally, it's enough to make me yelp.

"You had me worried I hadn't picked a big enough one for you," he says as he gives it a final push home, making me really scream.

"This afternoon, all your orgasms will be with an empty pussy. I want you to miss my cock inside you while you come."

Lying on top of me, he reaches between my legs and switches the Hitachi on, and no matter how hard I struggle to get away from it, he's pushing me back against it. I lose count of how many times he makes me come. Each orgasm slams into the next and all I can do is scream and cry and beg.

"No more, please, no more. I can't take anymore."

"You will take everything I give you or safeword like a good girl."

"Please, Sir. I can't."

He flips the Hitachi off, and before my clit can register the blissful peace, he flips the vibrator back on.

"You can. Eight more. Two for each punishment you earned."

"No, please. Anything else. Please, anything. I just can't."

"None of that was your safeword."

By the time he finally turns the vibrator off and releases me, I can't move. I'm nothing more than a floppy rag doll.

He lays down beside me and pulls me into his arms, his steady heartbeat soothing me as I drift off.

ELEVEN

Eli

"Up we get. It's supper time."

She rubs her eyes and smiles at me. "Oh. I wasn't dreaming, then."

"No, not a dream. Come on, sleepyhead. Let's go eat and I'll fill you in."

"I'm sure you will."

"That's one. That smart mouth of yours really gets you into trouble."

I lead her to the kitchen and point to her chair. I've thoughtfully stuck a large dildo to the seat for her enjoyment. Or maybe it's for mine.

She looks at me, the question plain on her face, but wisely, her mouth remains closed.

"Hesitation is the same as arguing. Now, sit."

She gingerly positions herself and slides down the dildo, wincing as her ass touches the wooden seat.

"Problem?"

"It's a little...big."

"Yet you took it all like a good girl."

"Yes, Sir."

"I hope you like spanakopita and Greek salad," I say as I bring our plates to the table.

"Yes, Sir."

"You may eat. For now, you may feed yourself, but there may be times I'll want to feed you by hand."

"Yes, Sir."

Calliope still has half a plateful when I take my last bite. Sliding my dish away, I grab hers, pull it in front of me, and push my chair back just a bit. I fish a condom from my pocket and tear open the packet with my teeth as I undo the front of my jeans. "Come here and sit on this while I finish feeding you." I roll the condom down my erection.

She rises slowly off the dildo and backs onto my rigid cock.

"No, sideways."

I hold my cock upright while she slides down on it.

Bliss.

Supporting her back with my right arm, I load the fork. "Open."

She doesn't hesitate, and my cock twitches inside

her cunt as her lips close over the mouthful of food I offer.

"Please, Sir. I'm full," She says when there's still slightly better than a quarter of her dinner left on her plate.

In this, I don't push. Forcing a sub to eat more than she wants is farther than I'm willing to go. Besides, I have no real sense of what her appetite is. Maybe when I have a better idea of that, I might feel a little more controlling about her food.

"Okay. You did well. Off you get. Can you find your way back to the dungeon?"

"I think so. But I can help clean up."

"No, thank you. It only takes a few minutes to load the dishwasher and wipe up. Now get your sweet ass back to the dungeon, face down on the bed with your legs spread wide and wait for me."

"Yes, Sir."

TWELVE

Calli

Eli wakes me with little kisses along my bare shoulder. "Wake up, sleepyhead. I only have three hours left to have my wicked way with you before we need to go meet Mel. But first, I want to inspect your ass."

Flipping over, I spread my legs even though he didn't ask. I know I shouldn't anticipate his wants and needs, but I can't imagine he'll be too upset.

"Mmm, looks good. Lots of nice purple stripes, yet still lots of space for new sets daily."

I didn't get a good look at my ass last night, so I hope he gives me enough time before we leave to admire his marks in the mirror.

"Don't worry, you'll get to have a good look once I'm done with you."

It's kind of spooky how he does that.

"On your knees and forearms, ass high."

I pop my knees under me and arch my back.

"Very nice."

The mattress shifts, and I hear a drawer open and close. I don't bother to look. It won't make any difference to what he's going to do to me, and sometimes I like it better when I don't know what's coming.

I hear a cap open and close, and then he's kneeling behind me, the tip of his cock pressed against my asshole.

"You've been such a good girl, I decided to use some lube for this first time. Just be aware I'm not always going to be so generous."

"Thank you, Sir."

He presses into me, harder and faster than he had with the plug last night, but not being as wide, he's easier to take.

"I won't always be this gentle with you, either. I will take all your holes as hard and fast and rough as my mood dictates. And as always, you'll take everything I give you or safeword like a good girl."

"Yes, Sir, thank you, Sir."

He pulls all the way out, then stabs his way back in making me yelp.

"That's what I like to hear. Don't hold back. I want it all."

He impales me tip to root over and over and over. I don't know how he can hold off his orgasm so long. His self-control borders on inhuman.

"Do not come," he orders. "You don't get to come until I say. And I want you on edge all day. I want you to go through every house today with just one thing on your mind. The dungeon. I want you to evaluate every room in every house as if it's going to be the dungeon I torture you in."

"Yes, Sir."

He slams into me harder and faster until I recognize the signs of his impending orgasm. I want to come so badly, and at this point, it would only take a word from him and I'd be helpless to stop it.

His final plunge is untold relief, as he empties himself into me.

"You have been such a good girl, Calliope. I'm very proud of you. For the rest of the day, until we return here, we are just Eli and Calliope. I won't top you while we're out, and you may run your smart mouth off as much as you like without consequence. However, back-talk or hesitation will earn you punishments. And I will be sure to let you know the count as they rack up. Because if there's one thing I'm coming to know about you, there's always an infraction. Now off you go to admire your marks and get ready."

"Thank you, Sir."

I head off to the bathroom to check out my backside. I'm a little disappointed he doesn't want to join me in the shower, but given he's not been able to keep his hands off me whenever we're in the same room, maybe it's for the best if we're to be ready in time to meet Mel.

THIRTEEN

Eli

NORMALLY, I hate house-hunting, but with Calliope, it's been fun. Maybe it's because we're not looking for me. Maybe it's because we're both evaluating each property with hot, kinky sex in mind.

Maybe it's just because I'm with her. I let that thought rattle around for a minute.

Whatever the reason, I'm thrilled that it's only half-way through the day when she finds exactly the right house. We go look at the rest of the houses on her list anyway, but she was sure the moment she saw it.

Truth be told, I knew it was the one, too. To the point of taking Mel aside and telling her to go ahead and make the deal.

After dinner, I send her to the dungeon, and when

I join her, she's on her back on the bench, waiting for me.

"What a good and obedient girl you are," I tell her as I buckle her into her cuffs and clip her to the bench.

I fuck her throat hard and she takes it like a champ, and deep down, I hope she never actually gets over the gagging and heaving because, sick fuck that I am, I find that hot.

As soon as I shoot my load down her throat, I take her to the bed and make her come until she's limp and happy.

"I have something to tell you, and I'm warning you now, anything but graceful acceptance will result in punishment. And as we've seen, I'm very, very good at punishing you in ways you really don't enjoy. Understand?"

"Yes, Sir."

"The house you decided to buy is yours."

"Excuse me?"

"It's yours. Free and clear. A gift."

FOURTEEN

Calli

A GIFT?

I stare at him, stunned. Horrified. Hurt.

Humiliated.

After all my efforts to shuck the public's perception of me—he flings me back into the role of Hollywood Whore without even a second thought.

"Are you crazy? I can't accept that. I'm not a fucking whore."

"Stop right there. You're at one. You really don't want add to that."

"Red." I jerk away from him. "Do you really not understand that if I accept the house from you, it's nothing more than the proceeds of turning a trick."

"Nobody has to know."

"There is no way it doesn't get out. And even if, in some alternate reality, that wasn't the case—*I'd* know."

"Calli..."

"No. We're done. That house is tainted. I want to go home," I remove the cuffs, drop them unceremoniously on the floor, and stomp across the room to my clothes.

I'M grateful there aren't any paps outside my door when I get home. I don't hold out hope for that lasting long once the news breaks of our split.

I managed to hold it together for the entire ride from Eli's Lair, but the moment my front door is closed, I sink to the floor and let myself cry.

How could he do it? I loved that little house. It was perfect.

And he ruined it.

Sure, he just thought he was being a good guy. But that's the kind of gift that screams Jezebel. And while I've never felt the need for a ring to symbolize a committed relationship, I've never seen myself as a bought woman.

My phone pings.

. . .

Eli: I'm sorry.

I ignore it and block his number. It was a mistake to get involved with him again.

My phone pings again.

Mel: We need to talk.

I want to ignore and block her, too. But that is beyond stupid. She didn't do anything wrong. So I pick up when she calls.

"Pretty sure there's nothing to talk about," I say before she can even say hello.

"And that's why, of the two of us, *I* am the fixer. So, buckle up and hear me out before you say shit you'll only have to apologize for later."

"Mel, I know you mean well, I do. But it's been hard enough coming back from being branded a whore in the public eye. Your agent dumps you. Nobody takes your calls. Acquaintances won't acknowledge you. Contracts broken thanks to fucking morality clauses. Reservations are lost. Invitations are revoked. The list is endless." I don't bother mentioning the number of times I'd been approached to spend some quality time on the casting couch.

"There is no way I will put myself in that position again. Truth means nothing and perception is everything."

"He was just trying to lighten the load a little for you. You've been screwed over so badly, and sometimes it's okay to let someone give you a leg up."

"I've done everything on my own steam Mel. From the A list to the blacklist, it's been me the whole way, and I don't need anyone, least of all, a man—Eli—to give me a *leg up*."

"I can respect that—I didn't get where I am from beneath a man, but I did have support. So just please remember, Eli cares about you, and wants what's best for you. And so do I."

"Thanks, Mel. I appreciate everything you're saying. But I need to go now."

"Call if you need me. I'll be here."

Not in a million years, because I know the only reason Mel cares is because Eli is footing the bill.

LATE THE NEXT MORNING, I wake to my phone blowing up with breaking news notifications. I click the link to a video on the entertainment news site and there's Eli making it official.

"We had some lovely times together, but we came to realize our paths were headed in different directions and agreed to remain friends." I snort at that last bit.

I'm on my own.

FIFTEEN

Eli

How FUCKING arrogant must I be to think that I could just punish Calli into accepting a gift. And on top of that, the fact that it didn't occur to me that giving her a house could and likely would be seen as some kind of pay-to-play.

In the days after my colossal fuck up, my texts to her continue to go unanswered until I finally get the message that she no longer wants anything to do with me and give up.

As much as I wish that maybe sometime in the future, we could find a mutually agreeable way for the house to be hers, I know that's never going to happen. Because she's right. It is tainted. So, I pull out of the deal and sweeten the pot for the owners for dicking them around.

In the meantime, I throw myself into prep for my next film. Why I took on a role that required me to learn to use a broadsword and ride a bloody warhorse, I don't know. But at least the time and energy required to attain enough skill with both to be convincing on screen keep me from being fully consumed by the loss of my sweet, adorable submissive. The woman I'm hopelessly in love with.

A week after Calli walked out on me, Mel calls.

"I can't help those who don't want to be helped Eli, no matter how much money you throw my way."

"Thanks for trying."

"Stay out of trouble."

"No worries there. By the time I'm done training for the day I'm not looking for anything other than my bed—for sleep."

"That's what I like to hear. Good luck on this film."

"Thanks, Mel. I'll try not to need you."

I disconnect the call and try not to worry about Calli. She's pushing everyone away, and that worries me. But like Mel said, you can't help those who don't want it.

SIXTEEN

Calli

ONE AFTERNOON, just over a week after Eli and I broke up, my phone rings. I don't recognize the number, so I let it to go to voicemail.

My outgoing message for those not in my contacts is a man's voice telling them to, "Please leave a message after the tone." Nothing to confirm for unknown callers that they've reached my number.

I grab an apple from the fridge and take a big bite when my phone alerts to a voice message.

"Calliope, dear. It's Auntie Gert. I need someone to come to the salon with me, and seeing as you've got plenty of time on your hands these days, you'll do. I'll be at your door in fifteen minutes. Be ready."

I try calling her back to politely decline, but the call doesn't even go to voicemail. Did she actually block me?

There are so many reasons I shouldn't go with her. But I ignore them all because when it comes right down to it, I really like her, and she's right, I do have plenty of time on my hands. So, I put on my shoes, grab my purse and wait outside for her to arrive.

As soon as I join her in the back of the car, she grabs my hand and gives it a squeeze. "I told him not to fuck it up. But did he listen? Of course not. Stupid boy."

"Auntie Gert, I have to be honest with you, Eli and I—the whole thing was pretend. We weren't really together. Just making it look like it to hype up the film."

She laughs so hard I worry she's going to have a stroke. "I knew that. I might be packing a few extra decades, but I'm not senile. But the thing is, I've also been around the block a time or two. And I can tell when there's something special."

"There really isn't." *I wish there had been.*

"Never mind about that now. We're nearly there. Come closer and smile," she says as she holds her phone up to take a selfie of us.

"Auntie Gert, you aren't uploading that to Instagram are you?"

"Of course I am! What's the point of having forty million followers if I don't provide them with content?"

I just about swallow my tongue when the driver pulls the car up in front of The Polished Beaver. I steal a look at Eli's great-aunt to see she's sporting a huge grin and a terrifying twinkle in her eye.

And now I'm scared to open my Instagram.

We're greeted as soon as we walk in the door. "Miss Simmons. So lovely to see you again. We have you for a trim and dye. Ms. Muir, we have you for mani-pedi, facial, and waxing."

I don't know whether to laugh or scream at the audaciousness of Eli's great-aunt. But it's definitely been a while since I've had a little pampering, so instead I face Auntie Gert and accept the gift. "Thank you."

"My pleasure, my dear. My pleasure."

I don't see Auntie Gert again until I'm finished all my treatments. And holy shit. It takes me a minute to recover from her mermaid hair. "It's gorgeous. Absolutely amazing."

"I figure at my age, I am ready for another mid-life crisis. This was a little easier on the body than the nipple piercings were with my last one."

This woman. This take-no-prisoners, don't-give-a-fuck-what-others-think woman. I want to be just like her when I grow up.

After a few more selfies to feed the Instagram beast, we leave the salon and into the waiting car.

"We should go day-drinking."

"Auntie Gert, I've just had hair ripped from some very sensitive places—"

"All the more reason. But I can see you're about done with the galavanting today. So, we'll save day-drinking for another time."

"This isn't a pity thing, is it?"

"Oh good god, no. I really enjoy your company and I don't give a flying fuck whether you're dating my Eli or Jude Anderson or Joe the electrician. And I don't give a flying fuck about your reputation or what people think they know about you or their judgements. Although I'd understand if you don't want to hang around with a rickety old broad like me. I wouldn't want to cramp your style or anything."

"You are such a manipulator. And honestly, it's more likely I'd cramp yours."

"You're good people Calliope Muir. And don't let anyone try to make you feel otherwise."

We arrive at my house, and just before I get out, she pulls me into a hug. "I know you're not ready to forgive him. I know I wouldn't be. But don't give up on him yet. I'll see you soon for that day-drinking, my girl."

"See you later, Auntie Gert. And thank you again for this afternoon. I had a really good time." I kiss her on the cheek and hustle out of the car feeling better than I have since Eli and I parted ways.

SEVENTEEN

Eli

As much as I love my Auntie Gert, I'm not in the mood for her eccentricities. But here she is, at my front door. And from her expression, there's no turning her away.

"Hello Auntie. How are you? The hair looks great."

"Don't you try flattering me. I'm still annoyed as fuck at you."

I stay silent. I know she's got plenty more to say, and I don't have anything remotely acceptable in my defence.

"Why yes, I'd love a scotch," she says looking pointedly at her hand, her fingers curled like she's holding a glass. Clearly, she's settling in for the long haul.

I pour us each a generous double of the forty-six-year-old Bunnahabhain. Not my best single malt, but more than good enough to keep her from feeling snubbed.

"I do love a good Islay single malt," she says after taking her first sip. "Now—what are you going to do about this situation between you and Calli?"

"Nothing. What we had going is over and done with. Moving on." Except I'm not. I miss her more than I ever thought possible.

"Bullshit. You know I'm not one to meddle, but..."

I nearly shoot whisky through my nose. "I think it would be good if you kept it that way. I appreciate that you've been spending time with her."

"Ah. So you have been following my Instagram."

"I have." And there's no way on the planet I'm going to think about all the dirty nasty things I wanted to do with Calli when I saw she'd been to The Polished Beaver. Not while I'm in the same room as Auntie Gert.

"She's a good girl, Eli." My great-aunt's eyes look a little watery and discomfort makes me shift my gaze elsewhere. I can't recall the last time, if ever, I've seen her so sensitive.

"I know she is," I say gently. "But no matter how good two people are, some things just aren't meant to be."

"I won't stop seeing her, you know." And there she is. That wonderfully belligerent aunt so dear to my heart.

"And I wouldn't want you to. It makes me happy knowing she has someone special in her life."

"She could have two special someones if you'd get your shit together. Grovelling can be very effective when done properly. Cunnilingus. That's also an—"

I don't hear the rest because my sinuses and nostrils are on fire, and I'm dripping whisky down my face.

EIGHTEEN

Calli

It's been two months since I walked away from Eli, and I've spent way too much of that time mourning the loss of our brief kinky dalliance, which is making me squirrelly as fuck.

On the plus side, the paps have found other, juicier prey to stalk, leaving me to come and go as I please.

They say the only way to get over a man is to get under another, so tonight, I intend to do just that.

I sit in my car in the parking lot of a skeevy little bar and peruse the offerings. Enough to choose from, and thankfully, Eli's profile doesn't show up.

I get out of my car, and as I approach the entrance, I'm grabbed from behind. A hand covers my mouth and my arm is wrenched up high on my back.

"Don't you fucking fight me. I've been waiting a long time for this. I'm going to take my hand away. If you scream, I will cut you right here. Now walk back to the parking lot."

"I think you've got the wrong person,"

"I'm sure that I don't. Now move."

He has to have me confused for someone else. Kidnapping fantasies don't appear anywhere on my profile.

"Let me go. Someone is expecting me."

"Yes, and that someone is me." The voice is familiar, but I can't quite place it. He wrenches my arm higher, and I move before he gets it to breaking point.

"I know exactly what filthy, dirty stuff you're into. It wasn't hard to set up a profile you'd hook up with sooner or later."

He pushes me towards a black, windowless panel van in a dark corner of the lot. And I know I'm screwed. I'm in a sketchy neighbourhood, there's nobody around, and the lighting in this parking lot is shit.

I struggle to get away, but I'm not dressed for a fight. The fuck-me boots with five-inch spike heels were a really big mistake.

But this is Fetwrk, and it's supposed to be mutually assured destruction. It occurs to me death could be one hell of a loophole.

I stop in my tracks, ignoring the pain in my arm and stomp my heel backwards, raking down his shin. Five-inch spikes might be shit for running, but they are stellar for shredding this fucker's leg. He screams in pain and I do it again, and I use my weight as leverage to escape his hold on me. Turning to face him, I discover with why his voice was familiar.

Felix Fucking Alexander.

Somehow, my anger gives me the strength to keep stomping and fighting him until he's on the ground and in too much pain to move.

Pulling my keys from my pocket, I beeline to my car and lock the doors behind me. *Then* I remember the fucking panic button. Why the hell hadn't I pushed it?

It doesn't matter. I've managed to save myself.

It's hours later by the time I finally feel like I've scrubbed enough of the filth off my skin to allow myself into the sanctity of my bed.

But I don't get there.

While I was in the shower, my phone exploded.

Again.

I don't want to look, but I can't help myself.

There's footage of me beating the shit out of Felix Alexander, and of course, none of it includes his role in the whole business.

Fuck. Me.

NINETEEN

Eli

I CAN'T BELIEVE my eyes as I watch the video of Calliope kicking Felix Alexander's ass over and over.

"Seymour."

"Mel. It's Eli Simmons. What the fuck is going on with Calliope?"

"She fired me. I've already told you I can't fix those who don't want me to fix them."

"Damn it, Mel."

"Eli, I am doing what I can without her cooperation, but it's limited. And there's fucking video of her committing the assault."

"You know as well as I do that there's got to be more to it than that."

"Again, I can only do so much without her cooperation."

"Does she at least have a decent lawyer?"

The long deep sigh from the other end of the phone is all the answer I need.

"Eli, she can refuse counsel. I can't force her to accept a good lawyer, and the reality is, she's proud. And I don't think she's got the funds for the kind of defence she needs."

"I don't care what you need to do to make it happen, but at least make her accept the best defence lawyer my money can buy."

"I'll do what I can, but I can't force her to accept help."

"Thank you. Any suggestions as to what I can do to help from my end?"

"Not yet. Let me meet with her again, and I'll see what, if anything, she's open to. I'll be in touch."

I disconnect and toss my phone on the table, watching it skid across the smooth surface while I try to rein in my anger.

I know she's proud, but I never would have taken her for too foolish to accept help when she really needs it. I understand her issue with the house, but this is her freedom she's gambling with.

And she's up against Felix Alexander. One of the most powerful movers and shakers in Hollywood. And it's only just confirmed for me that he's the asshole in that video. I'd had my suspicions, and I could have asked Calli. But I felt it was important for the decision to tell me about the video, or not to be entirely up to her. Damn that man. He already fucked her career, now he's about to fuck her entire life.

As much as I want to just fucking show up where she's being held and bail her out, Mel's already told me that's the worst thing I could do.

For both Calliope and me.

So, I sit here, waiting for news of any kind while I watch the infamous video on repeat and read the increasingly outrageous comments as they're being posted.

One of the more popular theories is that she's so down on her luck she's taken to turning tricks.

And I know damned well she's going to find that the most painful.

I don't think I've ever felt more impotent in my life.

TWENTY

Calli

THE SOUND of the door opening makes me look up.

Mel. Again.

"I thought I fired you."

She shrugs and takes the seat across the table from me.

"Here's the thing, Calli. I owe you a couple of apologies, starting with when that video hit. When it became clear that Janet wasn't going to call me to help you, I made all sorts of justifications for why I didn't just step in. And for that I am truly sorry. It's too late for me to fix that, but I'm hoping you'll let me help you with this. Me. Not Eli. Not his great-aunt. Me. One hard lesson I learned is to do the right thing, not the right thing for my business. The second apology is for not standing up to Eli about the house. I knew it was the wrong thing for him to do, but he pays me for my ability to fix things, not for advice on his love-life. So that's twice I've done you a disservice, and if I had those two things to do over again, with the knowledge I have now, I would absolutely have made very different choices.

"I'm not going to ask for your forgiveness. I'm just going to ask that you let me help you now."

I struggle to process everything she's said, but I keep going back to her mention of my former agent.

"What did you mean about Janet wasn't going to call you in to help me?"

"In all the years I've known her, she's never hesitated to call me when a client was in some trouble. No matter how trivial. So, I was shocked when I never got called about you and the video."

"I see. I'm going to have more questions about that at some point."

"Whenever you're ready, I'll be happy to answer all your questions. In the meantime, as regards the more pressing matter—let me help. Please?"

I don't like it, but I'm in seriously bottomless shit.

I nod. "Yes, thank you."

"Good. Hang on a sec." She walks across the room and opens the door. Another woman walks in and they both sit across from me.

"This is Kendall Solomon, and she'll be defending you."

"Ms. Solomon."

She smiles at me. "Just Kendall, please. Now, can you tell me what happened, Calli? The whole story."

"I went to that bar looking for a hookup."

"You have an app for that," Mel interjects.

"I was using the app. So was Felix."

Her eyes go wide and there's no mistaking the anger in them, but she nods, encouraging me to continue. But there's something there. More questions I'm going to need to ask.

"Before I got to the door of the bar, he grabbed me from behind and tried to force me to a black panel van in the parking lot. As you should have seen from the video, I wasn't exactly wearing my best getaway boots, which meant wrenching free and running wasn't an option, so I fought back with what I had to work with. Because there was no fucking way he was getting me inside that van."

"And, of course, the video only shows the part where you stomp his ass and run away."

"Yep. So, here I am, in serious trouble for defending myself."

"What did you tell the cops?"

"Nothing. I took my right to remain silent very seriously."

"And that's going to work in our favor," Kendall assures me.

"I don't want to involve Fetwrk," I say to Mel. "It was only the means to an end. If it didn't exist, Felix would have found some other way to get to me."

"We'll do what we can to keep it from being used in your defence, but if it's necessary, I will not hesitate. Of course, when we developed it, we hoped the nature of the app itself would keep it out of the legal system, but that didn't stop us from building in some safeguards. Don't worry about anything except exercising your right to remain silent. That means you don't talk to anyone about this except for Kendall and me. Attorney client privilege and all that."

"I'll be good."

Kendall pushes back her chair and stands. "I'll go work on getting Calli released."

When Kendall is gone, Mel takes my hand and locks her gaze on me. "It's going to be fine. This might take some time to fix, but you're going to be okay. Trust me."

I nod, but I have a hard time believing anything will ever be fine again.

TWENTY-ONE

Calli

As the car rolls through the gates of Eli's Lair, my relief from being released turns to disappointment that Eli won't be there.

I still feel strongly about not accepting the house he bought, and my reasons haven't changed. But rather than just politely refuse his gift, I basically cut off my nose to spite my face.

And instead of having safe, regular, off-the-charts kinky sex, I spent the past two months lonely as fuck. Then, the first time I get out there for a hookup, I narrowly escape a kidnapping and probably worse, courtesy of the biggest scumbag in Hollywood.

The universe is definitely trying to tell me something.

As soon as I'm though the door, I take my bag to one of the guest rooms. I'm eternally grateful to Mel for everything she's managed to do for me so far, and I feel like a total shit for having pushed her away, too. No matter how much you want to stand on your own two feet, when you're a Hollywood black-lister, you can't afford to turn away support of any kind. Something I'm learning the hard way.

Once I'm unpacked, I wander through the house. I tell myself it's nostalgia, but in truth, I'm looking for signs he's brought another sub here.

I avoid his bedroom, though. And the dungeon because if he has brought anyone here, those are the most likely places I'll see evidence of it. But if I'm honest with myself, the most likely reason I stay away from those rooms is because they hold the most vivid memories.

My growling stomach reminds me that I actually haven't had proper food since before my arrest. I'm both surprised and grateful to find the kitchen is fully stocked. I make myself some toast and marmalade.

Not exactly a balanced meal, but it's something in my stomach, and it's quick and leans to the side of comfort food. I'll make myself something more substantial once I feel a little more settled.

I take a big bite of my toast, pull out my phone, and

unblock Eli's number. It's well past time I acted like a fucking adult, and I owe him a thank you.

Calliope: Thank you. For everything. You are literally a life saver.

Eli: You're welcome. I believe in you. So please, do whatever Mel and your lawyer tell you. I want to do more for you, but only as much as you'll let me.

I don't respond because I have nothing worthwhile to say. I don't deserve his help. But I'm in too much trouble to do anything but accept it and say thank you.

I make two more pieces of toast, and then head to bed. I'm an exhausted, emotional wreck.

The downside to falling asleep in the early evening is waking up in the wee hours of the morning when it's still dark and scary. And I wish Eli were with me. Being here awake and alone in the middle of the night like this messes with my head.

And I have nobody to turn to.

Even if I did, I'm only going to freak them out by texting in the middle of the night.

I need some kind of comfort, and finally, I gather

up my courage to go into Eli's room, where I pull one of his t-shirts from his dresser.

My intention was just to cuddle with it, but I need more. I need it next to my skin, so I strip out of my pajamas and slip his t-shirt over my head.

It falls a little past my mid-thigh and is soft against my skin. Deciding against returning to the spare room, I slide beneath the covers on his bed, pull his pillow tight against my chest, and let myself cry.

TWENTY-TWO

Eli

THE NEXT MORNING, I want to text her, make sure she's okay. She didn't respond to my last text last night, and I don't know how to interpret that.

I don't want to push. I already made that mistake.

Instead, I throw myself into research for my next role. Shooting starts in three months, and this film is going to stretch me to the limit.

Three hours later, my phone alerts.

CALLIOPE: I know you're busy, but if you find you've got some spare time, do you think maybe you could visit?

Eli: Just tell me when.

Calliope: Now?
Eli: On my way.

IT TAKES FOREVER to get there. Traffic in LA is never good, but fuck me, of course there had to be an accident and no fucking way to detour around it.

Calliope is standing on the front stairs as I pull up. She's biting her lower lip, a sure sign she's nervous. She looks too thin.

"Hi." Her voice is quiet, a little breathy with just a hint of shakiness.

"Hey."

I want to pull her into my arms, but I need a better sense of where she is in her head before I touch her.

"I made dinner in case you're hungry," she says as I follow her into the house.

"I am, thank you."

Her eyes go wide as I head to my bedroom. Her concern makes me curious, so I continue through.

My bed is a mess. The quilt is crumpled where she's obviously thrown it off when she got up. My pillow is peeking out from beneath it, and one of my t-shirts is in a pile on her pillow.

My heart is bursting at the knowledge that she's missed me.

"Um...I uh..."

"Hush. I didn't put any limits on your use of the Lair. And quite frankly, I like that you've been sleeping in here. In my shirt."

Her blush is so damned adorable.

"Dinner is ready whenever you are."

"Thank you. Go ahead and dish up, I'll be right there."

Feeling in my pocket, I pull out the necklace. I didn't really have any kind of plan for giving it to her, but this is perfect. I place it on top of the shirt, where she should have no trouble finding it.

As I walk into the kitchen, there are plates waiting on the table. "Stroganoff. One of my favorites."

"I hope you like it."

I can't hold back the moan as I take my first bite. "This is so good."

Her blushing face reminds me that she doesn't take compliments well, something I'd really like to work on with her.

"Eli, I need to apologize. I'm really sorry for my behavior over the house. While I could never accept a gift of that magnitude, I was rude, and bitchy, and completely out of line."

"Stop. You don't need to apologize."

"Yes. I do.

"That's enough. I don't want you to be worrying

about anything. I just want you to look after yourself. That's it. Promise me."

"Eli—"

"Promise me. I've never asked anything of you outside the dungeon. Not once. I need you to promise me this."

"I promise."

"Thank you. I should get going."

"Do you have to go?"

"What are you asking?"

I know exactly what I want it to be, but I need the words.

"Can you stay with me? Maybe overnight?"

"I can." I assume she means in her bed—well, my bed—but even if she means the sofa, my answer wouldn't change.

"Would you...maybe..."

"Calliope, out with it. The worst that could happen is I say no."

"Eli, please, could we have a scene?"

Yes! "Are you feeling needy?"

"Yes, Sir."

"Go to the dungeon and get ready while I clean up."

She pops out of her chair and practically runs down the hall.

I take my time putting the kitchen to rights. I want

to keep her a little off balance. She's way too far inside her head.

When I enter the dungeon, she's positioned for the skull-fucking she's not getting tonight.

"You're a good girl, but I have something else in mind. Up you get."

I help her down and stand her in the middle of the room. "I think tonight is for rope."

She grins so wide she's all teeth, and I know I've made the right move.

Silk tonight. She needs to suffer, that much is clear, but I won't risk marking her. Not while there's any chance she could be required to expose any skin to the authorities. So nothing that could leave marks that will last more than a few hours.

I'm ridiculously happy to see she doesn't bear any other man's marks even as I mourn the loss of my own.

"Have you been a good girl while we've been apart?"

"Mostly, Sir."

"Define mostly, please?"

"I was looking for a hookup on Fetwrk that night."

"Ah. And had you done that often during those months?"

"No, Sir. That was the first time." I'm happy she'd held out that long.

I know damn well she wants to know what I've been up to, and I'll tell her. But in my own time.

I start with a chest harness, making sure to wrap her breasts so they stick straight out. "So pretty." I lean down, take one nipple in my mouth, and suck hard before giving it slight nip. I move on to do the same with her other breast, but I bite that one a little harder, making her suck in a sharp breath. "So very pretty."

I lead her to the bed. "On your back, knees bent so your heels touch your bum.

She obeys me without question, and I almost want her to hesitate or refuse because I want to punish her so badly, but it wouldn't be fair of me to punish her for the mess she's in, even though I'm sure she thinks she deserves it.

I wrap the rope around her thighs, ankles, and then between them, making sure they're tight and secure. "Calli, you let me know if anything starts feeling numb or tingly. No safewords. You just tell me straight up what the problem is, okay?"

"Yes, Sir."

Once I've got the frog-tie complete, I attach the loose ends of the rope to the chest harness, spreading her wide for my pleasure.

"I want you to cup your breasts and pinch your nipples. As hard or as gentle as you like—that's up to you. But you don't let go. If you do, I stop. Understood?"

"Yes, Sir."

As soon as she's pinching those gorgeous nipples, I settle between her legs and lap at her glistening pussy. "I've been wanting to do this for so long, but I had so many other things I wanted and needed to do with and to you, first."

I flick the tip of my tongue over her clit, sometimes fast, sometimes slow. I bite down just hard enough to get a reaction when she squirms. "Every time you do that, I'll bite harder than the last. Now behave and let me work."

I close my mouth over her clit and suck gently as I slide two fingers deep in her pussy, fucking her with them, dragging them over her G-spot as as I increase the suction on her clit. Before long, her breathing changes, and her muscles tighten. I know she's hoping for permission, but she won't get it. Instead, I withdraw my fingers and lay a gentle kiss on her mound.

Her whine is so damned adorable.

I press more kisses on her mound, and along her inner thighs until she's no longer on the brink. Then I start the whole, delightful process all over again.

"Please let me come, Sir," she begs after I've edged her a fourth time.

"No. Tonight, you don't get to come at all. Just frustratingly close. And I don't have anywhere to be tomorrow, so I can do this all...night...long.

Her groan goes straight to my cock, and all I want to do is pound her until we both explode with pleasure.

But I have a lot of orgasm denial to administer first.

TWENTY-THREE

Calli

WHAT THE FUCK was I thinking when I asked him to stay?

I'm half-crazy with need thanks to the eighteen quintillion nearly, but just not-quite-there orgasms he hasn't let me have.

"Please, Sir. Please, make me come. Just once. Please?"

"Oh, Calliope, how many times did you beg me in this very room not to make you come. Which is worse. Too much, or not enough?"

"Not enough, Sir. Definitely not enough."

He chuckles that evil little laugh of his. "I wonder what your answer would be if I made you come until you begged me to stop.

"Let's find out, shall we?"

Oh my fucking god. The Hitachi rears its ugly big bulbous head and Eli uses some rope to rig it tight against my clit.

"I think we need a little more power."

How the fuck can there be any *more* power than the damned Hitachi?

Holding up a vibrating egg not much smaller than his fist, he shoots me that evil grin of his as he lubes it up and presses it inside me.

My brain almost explodes when the Hitachi and the egg start at almost the same time and he's had me so fucking on edge all night, my first orgasm slams into me out of nowhere, and it's not long before I'm begging him to stop.

"You seem to be out of practice. You've not come nearly enough yet to warrant that kind of begging."

"I lied. I'm sorry, I lied. This is worse. This is so much worse than edging. Please, Sir. I can't take any more. I just can't."

"You'll take everything I give you like a good girl."

I'm so wrung out, I could pass out. The thought barely crosses my mind when the vibrations stop.

"Thank you, Sir. Thank you."

"Don't thank me yet. I'm not done with you. I've been without my favorite toy for weeks, and we have much to make up for." He rotates me so my head hangs off the side of the bed, and I know where this is going. "Open"

He fastens the ring gag, places a ball in my hand, and then he slides in slow and deep.

"I've missed this throat so very much. I wanted to do this without the gag, but I can't risk you biting me when I do *this*."

The vibrators come to life, and I'm ready to go insane.

"You don't get to stop coming until I come."

God, I truly don't know how much more I can take.

The orgasms take over early and often, and it's all I can do to catch my breath between strokes.

Then I feel it, that slight swelling just before he shoots down my throat. As soon as he stops pulsing, he turns off the vibrators and pulls out.

"You've been a very good girl. I know you're tired. I think you should sleep well tonight. Now let's get you unwrapped and into bed."

I'm mortified when we enter his bedroom and I see the state I'd left his bed. "Eli, I'm sorry. I—"

"Hush. It's all right. You won't be needing this," he says as he picks up his t-shirt off my pillow. "But I hope you'll accept this."

In his other palm is a delicate chain with a Celtic O ring. Knowing him, it's platinum. Regardless... "It's beautiful. But I—"

"It's not a house. It's something for you to wear, to touch when you need a boost. For you to know I'm there for you. Even when I can't be."

His words are what make the gift precious. I'm truly touched. "Thank you. Will you put it on for me?"

"Of course."

He stands behind me and fastens it around my neck. And damn if it doesn't feel like a collar.

"Now, into bed with you."

We climb into bed and he pulls my back tight against his front, his hands cupping my breasts.

"Thank you, Eli. For everything."

"My pleasure. Now sleep. I'm tired."

TWENTY-FOUR

Eli

I WAKE TO A SOFT, wet tongue laving my morning wood.

Calliope

We'd only ever woken together the once. I'd told her she was always to wake me with a blow job. Apparently, she's still on board with that.

Reaching down with both hands, I tangle my fingers in her hair, and take over. I'm not anywhere near as rough as I was last night. Partly because she could actually bite me. But mostly because I want there to be gentleness between us.

Whether I want it or not, I have an emotional attachment to her that's getting tighter. I want more, and I really want to see where this could lead.

I don't care if she's on the Hollywood black-list. Those brief weeks where we were 'dating' proved it didn't make any difference.

Not that I'd care anyway. I've got more than enough money to last ten lifetimes, and I'd happily give up my career for the right woman.

Holding her head still, I pump my hips in a steady rhythm until I'm close to coming, then I pull out of her mouth and finish by hand, shooting all over her tits.

"What a dirty girl you are. I think you need a shower."

She grins at me, and I drag her off for a thorough cleaning.

Nearly an hour later, we're in the kitchen making breakfast when my phone pings.

MEL: Are you at the Lair?
Eli: Yes.
Mel: Head to Jude's. NOW!

SHIT.

"Calliope, that was Mel. She says I need to leave right now. I'll be back as soon as I can, if that's what you want. But considering your current the situation, when Mel tells us to do something, we both need to do it."

"I understand. Go. I'll be fine. And yes, please come back as soon as you can."

Grabbing a piece of toast, I give her a quick kiss, and once I'm on the road, I call Mel.

"What the fuck?"

"I just got the heads up that paps are on their way. Someone tipped them off that you own that house. I'll take care of Calliope, but I needed you out of there and as much distance between the two of you as possible ASAP. Jude will be waiting for you at the The Moose and Lumberjack Bistro."

TWENTY-FIVE

Calli

MOMENTS AFTER ELI LEAVES, Mel calls.

"Okay, what's up?"

"The paps are on their way there. I'm working on a distraction, but until you hear otherwise, you need to stay inside and away from the windows, especially at the front of the house. I know they're supposed to be privacy glass, but let's not take any chances. That house needs to look like there's nobody there."

"No problem. Any idea how long?"

"Hopefully just a few hours, but be ready to bug out on no notice."

"Thanks, Mel."

"I'll be in touch."

Fortunately, I've not actually spent any time in the

front rooms of Eli's house, so I don't need to risk going into any of them to retrieve any belongings. I throw on some clothes, and once I've got all my things packed, I go to the dungeon, the only room in the house without windows, and wait.

Fortunately, I carry my ereader everywhere, so I had something to help distract me.

MEL: Car is thirty minutes away. Be quick.
Calli: Thank you.

MY GUT IS CHURNING as I wait by the door with my bags. This is where it all goes to shit if there are paps outside. When I hear the car on the gravel, I chance a peek outside. The driver gets out, holds the back door open, and Prince Duncan climbs out. Apparently, Mel doesn't mess around when it comes to distractions.

I race outside and as we pass, he touches my shoulder. "It's going to be fine."

I hurry to the car hoping he's right.

"There was no sign of anyone as I came into the compound, but that doesn't mean they aren't there, so stay low until I'm sure we're in the clear, Miss. The car is supposed to look empty leaving here." The driver closes the back door behind me and stows my bags in the trunk.

I feel ridiculous hunkered down in the back of the car. Everything about my life over these past months has been ridiculous.

"You can get up and buckled in now, Miss. It's all good," the driver tells me a few minutes later.

"Thank you. Where are we going?"

"Ms Seymour has a safe-house ready for you. But first, we're taking a long drive.

All of this craziness could have been averted if I'd kept my fucking mouth shut about Felix Alexander.

TWENTY-SIX

Eli

I'M NEARLY at the restaurant to meet Jude when Mel calls. "What now?" I snap at her as soon as I answer the call.

"Felix Alexander leaked the location of the Lair to the media. Tara Langston told him. Langston's career is now so destroyed, she'll be lucky if she can get a job at a fast food joint. She was smart enough to connect some dots, but stupid enough to think the reward for doing Felix a favour would outweigh the destruction I can rain down upon her."

I like to think of myself as a forgiving kind of man, but I have a vindictive streak. "Kill her career dead. She blew her one and only chance."

"I intend to do exactly that. In the meantime, stay

with Jude until I call with the all clear and an address for a safe-house."

"Thanks, Mel."

There are already a couple of paps loitering outside The Moose and Lumberjack when I arrive, and I walk past them and into the restaurant like they aren't even there.

The hostess instantly recognizes me.

"Right this way, Mr. Simmons. Mr. Anderson is waiting for you."

"Thank you."

As she leads me through the main room, I see Jude sitting at a table near the window nursing a beer with another on the opposite side of the table. All visible to the outside world.

"How long have you been waiting?"

"Five minutes, tops."

"Okay, good. This for me?"

He grins. "Yep. All part of the service. So...?" he prompts.

"It was that rat-fucker Felix Alexander who leaked the location of The Lair, information he received from a past mistake of mine. She violated the NDA she signed and vastly underestimated Mel's reach. The foolish thing thought doing Felix a solid was worth the risk."

"Hoo-boy. She's well and truly fucked."

"Yeah, at least she's going to get what she deserves. But that still doesn't fix the shit Calli's in."

"Mel will get it sorted out."

"I know. But it's hard to just sit here and do nothing."

"Hard, but not impossible."

"Fine. Distract me. What's new and exciting in your life?"

"Lis Green."

I nearly choke on the beer I'd just taken a swig of. "I beg your pardon?"

"I've been seeing Lis Green. We hooked up on Fetwrk and..."

"Okay, back up just a minute. How low did you have your compatibility set for that to be a thing?"

"Want to quit with the judgement, Eli?"

"Not judging. I've never seen you doing the Daddy Dom thing before, and you've kind of thrown me here."

"Until this app, it was a lot easier, and less risky, to find a play partner who wants to call me Sir than Daddy. Now, there's an app for that."

I snort and he just grins. We're nearly finished with our meal when Mel texts to let me know we're in the clear and to call her once I leave.

"I know you're anxious," Jude says, "but let's have dessert and coffee before we split. Let the paps think you're not in any hurry to be anywhere."

We drag our meal out for another hour before we go our separate ways.

Once I'm on the road, I call Mel, and she gives me directions to a place in Beverly Hills along with the gate code. Even though I didn't see any paps when I left the bistro, there would be at least one or two who'd stay behind, just in case. I drove straight to my house first, and sure enough, I had one on my tail. He peeled off when I was within a few blocks of my house, and as soon as he was out of sight, I took the next turn and worked my way to the address Mel had given me in the most circuitous route possible.

She's waiting for me when I arrive.

"Calli should be here soon. I've got her driver taking her all over hell's half-acre to be sure she's not followed."

"Yeah, I did pretty much the same. What is this place?"

"The house I grew up in. It's the safest place I could think of for you two to hole up. Come on, I'll show you around while we wait."

TWENTY-SEVEN

Eli

AFTER SHOWING me around the safe-house, Mel got a call and had to leave. To be honest, it was a relief. My patience is worn clear through, and I'm not good company.

Calli should be here by now, and I won't relax until I have her in my arms and can see for myself that she is fine.

As soon as I hear the crunch of tires on the gravel driveway, I race to the front door and yank it open.

Seconds later, Calli exits the back of the car looking tired and worn.

"Thank you," she says to the driver as he pulls her things from the trunk.

"You're welcome, Miss. Take care."

As soon as we are in the house and the door is closed, I pull her into my arms and kiss her.

"Are you hungry?" I ask.

"Starving."

"Come on, sweetheart." Grabbing her ass with both hands, I lift her up and once she wraps her legs around me, I take her straight to the kitchen and set her on one of the stools at the island. "You can drink wine while I make dinner. Sound good?"

"Sounds great. I haven't had a proper meal since last night. But damn, you do keep good snacks in The Lair, and I sure appreciated it."

"I'll make a note to keep every place I own well-stocked with good snacks in case of paparazzi siege." And hope to fuck we never need them.

In the kitchen, I start by opening a bottle of red and pouring a glass each for Calli and me. "Do you want something to snack on while I cook?"

"No, thank you. I can wait."

Opening the fridge, I do a quick inventory to see what I can have ready to go fastest.

"How about chicken breasts with broccoli and mashed potatoes?"

"So good."

I pull the chicken and broccoli from the fridge and pop them on the counter before grabbing a few potatoes from the bin in the pantry.

"Can I help?" Calli asks as I start peeling potatoes.

"Yes. You can sit right there looking gorgeous and chat with me about inconsequential things."

"I feel useless watching you do all the work."

"Sweetheart, I've felt useless for weeks. Finally, I have something I can do for you. Please don't take that away from me."

"Fine, you want chatter about inconsequential things? I can do that. Tell me all the latest really good gossip—that isn't about me."

I chuckle. "How about inside news?" I'm sure Jude will forgive me for this.

"Oooh, even better. Spill."

"Jude has a woman."

"Oh please. Jude *always* has a woman."

"Seriously, he *has* a woman."

"Oh my god, like someone more than a passing fancy?"

"So much more. And he's terrified she's going to get crucified by the paps."

"Have you met her?"

"Yes, but not in this capacity."

"Do I know her?"

"Lis Green."

"Excuse me? Did you really just say *Lis Green*?"

"I did."

"Huh. I never took Jude Anderson for a Daddy Dom."

"Yeah, well…As he put it, now there's an app for that."

"That's some serious juicy. And yeah, I can see how he'd be worried about the press getting hold of that tasty morsel."

Just as I put the potatoes on to boil, Calli's phone rings.

TWENTY-EIGHT

Calli

My heart races, I'm so terrified at what Mel might have to say. My life has been nothing but bad news for months, and I'm not sure I can handle any more. I focus my gaze on the phone. I can get through this if I just focus on that.

"We lucked out, big time on those so-called assault charges," she says, excitement in her voice. "Apparently, there's been problems with people coming out of that bar and causing trouble at the shop directly across the road, so the owners have cameras set at different angles, including one aimed across the street. That camera caught the whole thing."

"Why didn't the owners come forward with this?"

"They didn't think about it. They only check the footage when there's been a problem with their own property. Wil did a thorough check of the area and spotted it. It's not obvious, and I guess the cops figured they had all the evidence they needed to convict you, so they didn't look any further. Anyway, fortunately for us, the shop has good quality cameras that broadcast directly into the cloud. So the footage is clear and preserved. We just have to decide how best to use it."

"What does Kendall say?" I ask.

"I haven't talked to her. I wanted to discuss this with you, first."

"Okay. If it were you...?" I ask

"I should say, *but it's not me*. However, I want to nail this cocksucker dead to rights. So, if it were me, I'd take that footage to the police and press charges. I'd also make sure there were copies that maybe got leaked to the media. Kind of like that footage of you kicking his ass did. Because I wouldn't be surprised if that might help others he's fucked over to come forward. But that's me. There is also the option of just sitting tight and producing it at your hearing to have the charges dismissed."

"What would happen with him if we just used it to get my charges dismissed?"

"Honestly, I don't know. But I wouldn't be

surprised if nothing came of it. He'd probably make some kind of deal to keep it buried. But the decision has to be yours. If you press charges—"

"California has revenge porn laws, right?"

"Yes. But they're misdemeanors."

"They're still criminal charges, though, right? He'd have to stand trial?"

"Yes."

"And every charge we bring against him is one more thing that can draw out other victims?"

"Yes."

I take a big breath, let it out slowly, and give myself a few moments to gather the courage and strength for what comes next.

"Then I want to go after him. He's already destroyed too much of my life, I don't have anything more to lose. Do what you need to, Mel. I'm going to fight."

"I'll call Kendall and make the necessary arrangements. It's going to be fine."

"Thank you, Mel. I appreciate everything you've done."

"Enjoy the rest of your night."

"You, too."

Mel disconnects, and I finally let myself look at Eli.

"Hey. Are you up for this? Truly?"

I nod. "Yes, I believe I am. It's time for me to stand up for myself."

"You don't have to stand alone."

EPILOGUE

Calli

The thaw was slow to start. Even with charges hanging over his head, and more victims coming forward, Felix still wields enough power to keep most producers and directors, particularly the men, from hiring me.

But after Kit Jamieson, actress-turned-director and fellow Felix survivor, reached out and offered me a role in her upcoming rom-com, it's been better. Kit's not ready to come forward—for now, she told me she's more comfortable providing support however she can for those of us who have.

Eli is on location in England brandishing broadswords and riding warhorses. I hate being apart, but we manage to steal time together. He's due home in a few days, but this is too good to wait.

I check the time and decide that it's not too late to call.

"Hi sweetheart. Everything okay?" he asks when he answers his phone.

"I have news."

"Don't make me wait."

"Miles Remesz has asked me to costar."

"Didn't he say you'd never work on one of his productions?"

I believe his exact words were, *I'd never allow your amoral, perverted, deviant soul to defile any of my productions.* "I guess he wants Meredith Carr more than he doesn't want me."

"Are you considering it?" He's concerned, but careful to stay neutral. He made it clear ages ago that he would never stick his nose into my professional life.

"I'm going to do it. But only because Meredith contacted me first. She wants to do this film so badly, but not without me. And Remesz wants *her* so badly he agreed to strike out the morality clause in my contract. I don't know—I feel honor-bound to do it on that point alone."

He chuckles. "As long as it's what you want to do."

"It is. And I love you."

"I love you too, Calli. Only three days until I fly home to see you. I don't suppose you've spent my absence moving my stuff into your house?"

"No..."

"Yours into mine?"

This is it. Time to commit.

I take a big breath and hold it for a few seconds to slow my heart down.

"Calli?"

"I had a different plan."

"Oh?"

"I was thinking of something else. We should go hunting for *our* house."

He repeats the last two words, and they sound even better in his voice.

"Our house."

Yes. I love the sound of that.

THE END

ACKNOWLEDGMENTS

Susan Hayes for Chix 'n Cars along with the innumerable other awesome ways she supports me.

Zoe York for another awesome cover, always being willing to brainstorm with me when I ask, and helping me unstick the epilogue.

Tymber Dalton, for brainstorming and hand holding.

Danny for some neighbourhood stuff - anything I got wrong, blame him. (He won't mind, I still owe him for his part in the 5am visit from Welsh police back in 1986).

Jana Aston for convincing that The Polished Beaver is really salon, not a bistro.

Jean Siska for all things legal. As always, anything I got wrong is 100% on me because I'm perfectly happy to bastardise reality if it gets in the way of the story.

Vera and Nancy for being amazing beta readers who catch the things I miss! Thank you, my lovelies.

As always, my truly lovely Dayna Hart who one day will get fed up with my panic books and dump my ass.

And finally, my husband for accepting that crazy is part of my process.

ABOUT THE AUTHOR

Surrounded by mist-covered mountains, Sadie Haller lives a quiet life with her husband and fur-babies.

Where to find Sadie
sadiehaller.com
sadie@sadiehaller.com
Follow on Bookbub

www.ingramcontent.com/pod-product-compliance
Lightning Source LLC
Chambersburg PA
CBHW010511100726

47902CB00011B/2170